STAR GAZING

STAR GAZING

Kate Thompson

BBC
LARGE
PRINT

First published in 2008 by
New Island
This Large Print edition published
2009 by BBC Audiobooks
by arrangement with
New Island

ISBN 978 1 405 62250 9

British Library Cataloguing in Publication Data available

Printed and bound in Great Britain by
CPI Antony Rowe, Chippenham, Wiltshire

CHAPTER ONE

The bride was in white satin. She had a tiara on her shiny blonde hair. Her make-up was perfect. Her manicure was flawless. She was posing next to a vase full of stargazer lilies. She looked fabulous.

Daisy O'Donnell turned the page of the glossy magazine. The next photo showed the bride with her bridesmaids. Oh dear. Why had the poor girls allowed themselves to be dressed in lavender satin? They looked like badly wrapped presents. They looked like the kind of presents you wouldn't even want to unwrap.

It must have been the bride's plan, Daisy thought. She had picked out horrible dresses for her bridesmaids so that she would look perfect next to them. Daisy decided she would never do that. She would never dress her bridesmaids in ugly clothes. She

1

would never make them wear strapless gowns that showed their fat arms. And she would certainly never make them carry such nasty flowers. Lavender and yellow roses! If Daisy ever married, she would get married barefoot on a beach. With daisies in her hair . . .

'Daisy! Get a move on! Those flowers are due to be picked up by lunchtime. It's after twelve o'clock now.'

'Sorry, Mam. I was checking out the wedding flowers in *VIP*.'

'What? What are you on about?'

'*VIP* magazine!' Daisy slid the magazine across the counter. 'They have a section on weddings every month,' she explained.

Her mother, Rose, took one look at the lavender and yellow blooms. 'Tacky,' she said. 'Bog-standard stuff. Now, look at the work of art *you* are putting together, Daisy. You just get better and better.'

Daisy was arranging a bunch of

2

cream roses and glossy laurel leaves. Here and there were dotted tiny pearls. 'I learned everything I know from you, Mam,' she said.

'Thank you, love. You say all the right things.' Rose moved to the window and looked at the view of the harbour. 'Jack Coyle is back from his fishing trip. Fancy fresh fish for supper?'

'Sounds good.'

'I'll bring back some crab claws, too. We can have them for lunch.' Rose wound a red velvet scarf around her neck. Then she grabbed her bag and went out the door. Daisy heard her singing, 'Oh, I do love to live beside the seaside!' as she went down the steps.

Daisy watched her mother through the window as she strode towards the harbour. Now in her late forties, Rose was still a striking woman. Heads turned when she walked down the village street. Americans in tour buses stared. People in the village

3

wondered if she would ever marry again. But both Daisy and Rose knew that would never happen.

Daisy had watched her mother at work in the flower shop since she was a little girl. It had seemed natural to join her there after Daisy left school. Rose and Daisy were that rare team—a mother and daughter in perfect harmony. They had the same taste in music. They shared the same sense of humour. They even borrowed each other's clothes from time to time.

Rose's shop had once been an old-fashioned corner shop. That was part of its charm. Customers loved the wooden counter. They loved the fire that Rose lit in winter in the cast-iron fireplace. And they loved the air of friendliness about the place.

The shop was on the main street of the little village of Rosscrana. Rosscrana was the kind of village you might see on a postcard. In fact, visitors to the village bought postcards by the dozen. The most popular one showed boats bobbing in the harbour under a brilliant blue sky. People who came to Rosscrana often said how much they would love to live there. But the visitors came in the summer. They didn't know what it was like to live in the village in winter. In the winter, harsh winds blew in from the Atlantic.

The B & Bs shut down. The restaurants and cafés closed their doors. And business in Rose's shop was very quiet. Thank God for the insurance money that saw them through those times. The insurance money was the only good that had come out of Daisy's father's death. He had died three winters ago. Rose had planted snowdrops on his grave.

In winter, Daisy dreamed of moving to the city. She dreamed of shopping in posh places like Brown Thomas. She dreamed of clubbing in hip places like Lillies Bordello. She dreamed of dining in the restaurant of the Hamilton Hotel. She had read somewhere that the wine list there should come with a loan offer!

But she also knew that if she moved away from Rosscrana, her mother would miss her badly. Since Daisy's father had died, Rose suffered from panic attacks. Daisy minded her mother when the attacks happened. She put her to bed. She got her pills. She ran her baths and washed her hair. And she kept the shop up and running. Moving to the city would never be more than a dream for Daisy.

The phone rang. It was Mrs Darcy's housekeeper with an order for two floral arrangements. The fancier the better, said the housekeeper. Money was no object. Mrs Darcy was giving a dinner party. She wanted her table to look as classy as possible. Whatever Mrs Burke had paid for her flowers last week, Mrs Darcy would double it. The housekeeper added that *very important people* would be at the dinner party. Business clients of Mr Darcy's, probably. Mr Darcy was a developer who was so rich he had his own helicopter.

Daisy sighed and reached for the barrier cream. Working as a florist meant that she had to take great care of her hands. All the contact with water dried them out. All the trimming of woody stems made them rough. All the binding with twine gave her blisters. Sometimes she treated herself to a manicure in the local beauty salon. But not often. Manicures were expensive.

As she rubbed the cream into her hands, she looked at the cover of *VIP.* Two Irish soap-opera actresses were smiling back at her. Jane Clark and Mags Mooney were two of the brightest stars of *Ardmore Grove*—a television soap. On the cover of *VIP*, Jane and Mags were hugging so their cheeks touched. How glamorous they were! They had teeth straight out of a toothpaste ad. They had swishy hair and glowing skin. They were wearing clothes that were probably designer. Daisy bet that Jane and Mags shopped in Brown Thomas. She bet that they clubbed in Lillies and dined out in the Hamilton. She bet that they snacked on champagne and caviar.

Daisy had learned from last week's *Rosscrana Gazette* that *Ardmore Grove* was to film an hour-long episode in the village. The storyline had two of the *Ardmore Grove* families renting a holiday cottage by the sea. The *Gazette* had also announced a picture phone-in competition to tie in with filming. One lucky winner was to appear in the episode as a 'special' extra. The prize included lunch with the cast and signed photos of all the stars. Everyone in Rosscrana fancied their chances of getting in front of the cameras. She had heard that some had even put the competition phone number on speed dial so they could send in their photo again and again.

Of course Daisy had entered the competition. But she didn't have a snowball's chance in hell of winning. Daisy never won anything. Well—she had won a tin of biscuits in a raffle once. But when she had got the biscuits home, she had found that they were past their best-before date.

Sometimes she felt that she was heading for her best-before date too, hanging round in a village while life passed her by. She lifted a bucket full of stargazer lilies onto the counter. Some water slopped out onto the cover of *VIP.* The TV stars on the cover looked up at her as if put out. She held their gaze. Hah! When her mother named her after a flower she should have called her Lily, not Daisy. Stargazer lilies were among the most popular flowers in the shop. But the only stars Daisy was ever likely to gaze on weren't those who appeared in films or on TV. They were the ones that hung in the night sky over Rosscrana. Where nothing ever happened.

CHAPTER TWO

The bell above the shop door rang. A middle-aged woman walked into the shop. She had red cheeks and warm brown eyes. 'Hello there, Daisy!' said Katie Conroy.

'Good morning, Katie,' said Daisy. 'How's it going?'

Katie Conroy and her husband, Peter, owned the village store. Conroys' sold firelighters and 'fancy' goods. It sold sausages and hand-made chocolates. It sold Sunny Delight and fine wine. It sold *Ireland's Own* and *Cosmo*. Because it was the only shop of its type in the village, everybody shopped there. So of course Katie Conroy knew everything about everyone. But Katie was no gossip. And she was as wise as she was discreet.

'Things are going great,' said Katie. 'God is in his heaven. All is right with the world. And I'm here to order a couple of big bunches of flowers from you.'

'Celebrating something?'

'Yes. It's my mother's birthday next weekend. All the Conroy clan will be coming for a big family dinner.'

'All of them? The out-of-towners too?'

'Yes. Ger and Tina and Vincent are coming by bus. And Cal is flying into Galway.'

Daisy dropped her eyes and started playing with a pin. 'Are they staying for the whole weekend?'

'They are. Apart from Cal. His course is finished, so he is back for good.'

'Oh?' Daisy tried not to sound too interested.

'He has decided to start up his own business here in Rosscrana.'

Cal—Katie's youngest son—had left the village three years ago. He had gone to London to study carpentry. At the time, Daisy had told him he was mad. 'What do you want to do carpentry for?' she had asked him. 'Why not go into computers or web design? Carpentry is *so* last century, Cal.'

'And *floristry* is the new rock 'n' roll?' He had raised an eyebrow at her. But Daisy could think of nothing to say to that. And when he had called round to say goodbye she had pretended not to be at home. She didn't know why, but she felt that saying goodbye to Cal might not be easy. They had known each other forever. She even had a memory of Cal pushing her in her buggy when she was a toddler. He had pushed her so fast across the playground that she had fallen out.

'Cal is setting up a business, is he?' Daisy asked Katie. 'Something to do with carpentry, I guess?'

'That's right. He has already got a job from the Darcys. They want him to build a big entertainment unit.'

Katie's voice was full of pride.

'Katie! How are you?' Rose had breezed back into the shop. She was carrying a big paper bag that smelled of the sea.

'I'm grand, I'm grand,' said Katie. 'I was just telling Daisy that the whole family will be here next weekend.'

'I'd heard that. Great excitement. Will Cal be bringing his fiancée?'

Daisy was glad that her phone rang at that minute. She didn't want to hear about Cal's English fiancée.

'Hello,' said a voice when Daisy pressed 'talk'. 'Is that Daisy O'Donnell?'

'Speaking,' said Daisy.

'Daisy, my name is Ann Malone. I'm a PA on *Ardmore Grove*.'

'Oh?' Daisy's heart started to beat a little faster.

'I'd like to congratulate you, Daisy. You have won our phone-in competition to appear as an extra on the show!'

'*I* have?' said Daisy. 'But I never win anything!'

'Well, you've struck lucky this time,' said Ann. 'You'll be joining the cast for a day's filming next week.'

'That's amazing!' said Daisy. 'Believe it or not, I'm looking at two of the cast on the cover of *VIP* right now!'

'Jane and Mags? Well, you'll be thrilled to know that all of your scenes will be with them.'

Daisy was lost for words. She gazed down at the photograph of the two smiling soap-opera stars, feeling shocked.

'Daisy? Are you still there?'

'Yes! Yes, I am.'

'We would like to see you in make-up at eight o'clock sharp on this day week.'

'In make-up? You mean you want me to do a full make-up job on myself?' Daisy was horrified. She would never be able for glossy hair and glowing skin like Mags and Jane.

15

She could hear the smile in Ann's voice. 'No, no. One of our make-up girls will take care of you. We'll be setting up a make-up room in the village hall. Let me have your e-mail address. I'll send you the call sheet.'

Daisy gave her the address.

'Oh—and I'll need to know your dress size,' added Ann. 'I'll send you a form to fill in. Wardrobe will want to kit you out in something glam. You'll be in a dinner party scene with Mags and Jane. You won't want to let the glamour-puss side down!'

'Oh, no. Of course not!' Oh—*help*!

'Goodbye, Daisy. Look forward to seeing you next week!'

Daisy put the phone down on the counter next to *VIP*. Jane Clark and Mags Mooney were still smiling up at her. Her new best friends! And this time next week she would be having her face made up by a professional make-up artist! 'Wardrobe' would be dressing her up in something glam!

And she would be lunching with the stars!

She looked up at her mother and Katie Conroy.

'What was all that about?' asked Rose.

Daisy did a little dance and hugged herself with glee. 'I'm gonna live forever!' she sang. 'Baby—remember my name!'

'What *are* you on about?'

'They're the lyrics from "Fame".'

'What has that got to do with anything?'

'I'm going to be on the telly!'

Katie looked shocked. 'You've never won that *Ardmore Grove* competition!' she said.

'I have! Yay! Lights. Cameras. Action!'

Her mother looked unimpressed. 'It's far from lights and cameras you were reared, Daisy O'Donnell. And as for action—those flowers should have been ready half an hour ago.'

But there was a smile hovering

around the corners of her mouth.
And Daisy knew she was pleased.

CHAPTER THREE

The next Monday morning, Daisy made her way to the village hall. Her call was for eight o'clock, but she had set her alarm for half past six. She had wanted time to do something with her face and hair. Even though she knew the make-up girl would be doing her up later, she didn't want to arrive looking like a frump.

Big trucks were parked outside the local restaurant—The Staff of Life. Men were carrying equipment through the restaurant door. A carpenter was hammering at a window frame. A man in a yellow jacket was barking orders into a phone.

Daisy had learned that the scene she was to appear in was being filmed in The Staff of Life. Ann Malone had told her that it was a party scene. She would be sitting at a table with Mags and Jane and some other cast members 'enjoying dinner'. Daisy knew she wouldn't be able to eat a thing. Her tummy was full of butterflies.

'You're Daisy, aren't you?' A woman was walking towards her. 'I recognise you from the photograph you sent in. No one could mistake that lovely red hair!' The woman held out her hand. 'I'm Ann Malone. We spoke on the phone. Nice to meet you, Daisy.'

'Likewise!'

'Come with me,' said Ann with a smile. 'We'll see what wardrobe has picked out for you.'

Together they walked down the path and into the hall. It had been divided up with tall screens. 'Make-up is over there.' Ann pointed left. 'And wardrobe is behind here.'

She led the way around one of the screens. Costume rails had been set up in rows. Most of the clothes were pretty ordinary. But one rail had lots of beautiful dresses. There were romantic dresses in floral prints. There were posh dresses in silk. There were glamorous dresses in satin. And wardrobe had picked out a dream of a dress in chiffon for Daisy. It was the kind of dress you would want to do twirls in.

And after she had slipped it over her head she *did* do a twirl. The wardrobe lady smiled and picked a piece of lint off Daisy's hem. 'You're lucky to be in a party scene,' she told her. 'Extras don't often get the chance to look this glam. Now off you go to Lisa in make-up. Be sure to let her know if you've any allergies.'

Luckily, Daisy had none. And when she looked in the mirror half an hour later, a different person looked back at her. Her skin was dewy. Her lips were glossy. Her black-lined eyes were smoky and mysterious. She could have walked off the cover of *VIP*!

'Thank you so much!' she told Lisa. 'You've worked a miracle! I've never felt so glamorous.'

'All in a day's work,' said the miracle-worker. 'Ah—here you are!' she added as two women appeared around the screen. They were Mags Mooney and Jane Clark.

Daisy almost didn't recognise them. They looked nothing like their photographs in *VIP*. Mags's normally sleek hair was frizzy. She was running a cordless GHD over it. Jane had a headful of big lumpy rollers. She was wearing jeans and a baggy sweater. Mags was wearing a T-shirt that read 'Stuff Art, Let's Dance'. Neither of them was wearing make-up. They looked dog tired. But their smiles were friendly.

Lisa the make-up girl performed introductions.

'Hi,' said Jane, holding out a hand.

'Nice to meet you,' said Mags.

Lisa slid the make-up cape from Daisy's shoulders. 'Sit down over there and relax,' she told her, pointing at a chair. 'Ann will come and fetch you when they're ready to rehearse.'

Feeling shy, Daisy sat stiffly on the chair. She didn't want to crease her lovely chiffon. As well as the dress, wardrobe had given her a shrug and a pair of heels. The straps on the heels were so thin they felt barely there. She kept looking down at her feet so she could admire them.

'Who's first for make-up?' Lisa asked the pair of actresses.

Jane yawned. 'It had better be me,' she said. 'Otherwise you will have to put matchsticks in my eyes to keep them open. I only got three hours' sleep last night. I'm *so* tired.'

She was probably out dancing until dawn, decided Daisy. Drinking expensive fizz in one of those clubs she read about in the gossip columns.

'Baby still teething?' Lisa asked Jane.

'Yep. And he has a bad case of

23

nappy rash as well. Double trouble.'

Mags slid into the seat beside Daisy. 'Jane has a one-year-old,' she explained. 'And her partner's away right now. She has to mind him all on her own.'

'Oh. Poor her.' Daisy's vision of Jane knocking back champagne in some nightclub bit the dust. She looked over at the actress slumped in the make-up chair. There was a stain on the back of her T-shirt that might have been baby sick.

Mags reached into her big bag and took out a script. 'Mind you, I'm pretty tired myself,' she said. 'It took me hours to learn my lines last night.'

Daisy looked down at the thick script. There were lines upon lines of dialogue. 'How on earth do you remember all those words?' she asked.

'With difficulty,' said Mags. 'These episodes are rubbish. Badly written stuff is much harder to remember than well-written dialogue.'

'Really?'

'Yes. And my concentration is gone at the moment. I keep thinking about formatting and tables.'

'What?'

'Formatting and tables. I'm doing a course in web design.'

'Really? As a hobby?'

'No. I want to be able to make a living from it.'

Daisy's mouth fell open. 'But—but *why*? I would have thought you had the best job in the world!'

Mags gave a little laugh. 'That's what everyone thinks,' she said. 'Everyone thinks that being in a soap opera is pure glamour. Believe me, it's not. It's hard going. For the past six weeks I've been working twenty-four seven.'

'You mean you don't even get Sundays off?'

'I spend Sundays studying scripts.'

'That *is* tough.'

'It gets worse. When I get home at

night I have to learn lines for the next day. I prop the script up on the kitchen table while I eat my dinner. And then I fall into bed. Far from glamorous.'

'But don't you get to go to a lot of parties and stuff?'

'With a schedule like that? Are you kidding?'

'But you're always in the gossip columns of the Sunday newspapers!'

'I go to fancy events when I'm not involved in a storyline,' said Mags. 'But to be honest, I'd rather stay at home with a good book or a DVD.'

'No! Really?'

'No word of a lie.'

'Then why do you bother going to the fancy events?'

'It's political. The more column inches you get in the paper, the more episodes you get. And I need the work.'

'Why do you get more episodes if your name appears in the paper?'

'The powers that be notice. They

think: "Oh, Mags is getting publicity. People want to read about her." And if people want to read about me, they must want to see me on the telly, too. So I get written into more episodes. And more episodes means more money. It's as simple as that.'

Daisy was amazed. She had always thought that Mags Mooney and Jane Clark led such charmed lives!

'Coffee's up!' Ann Malone came around the side of the screen. She was carrying a tray. On it were plastic cups, a flask and a carton of milk. There was also a bag of sugar and a packet of Marietta biscuits. And to think that Daisy had thought that actresses snacked on champagne and caviar!

Jane groaned from the make-up chair. 'Keep me away from those biscuits,' she said. 'I'm still half a stone overweight.'

Mags reached for the biscuits. 'The camera adds half a stone,' she told Daisy in a low voice. 'And poor

Jane hasn't lost her baby weight.'

'Can't she go to the gym?' Daisy asked. 'I heard that worked for Geri Halliwell.'

Mags gave Daisy a sideways look. 'The gym would be a fine thing!' she said. 'Jane barely has time to go to the loo.'

'I'm ready for you now, Mags,' said Lisa.

Mags stood up. She reached for another Marietta.

'You have a lovely figure, Mags,' said Daisy. 'How do you keep it that way?'

Mags gave a laugh. 'Stress,' she said.

CHAPTER FOUR

'And . . . *action*!'

Daisy was sitting in a corner of The Staff of Life. She was waiting for the floor manager to cue her. They had been filming in the restaurant for two hours. Powerful lights had been set up. It was hot and stuffy. The small space was crowded with actors, extras, crew, wardrobe people and props men.

After each take, a make-up girl would dash up to the cast members. She would pat with a powder puff here, dab with a lip brush there. Daisy thought it was odd to see the men being made up. Especially since three of them were so macho.

The main cast members were all sitting round a big table. They had just learned that another character in the soap had died. Two of the actresses were open-mouthed.

Others were comforting each other. Daisy was impressed to see real tears on Mags's face.

Daisy looked at the floor manager. She was counting down. She knew her cue was coming up in around thirty seconds . . . twenty seconds . . . ten . . .

Now! The floor manager pointed at her. This was her signal to walk across the restaurant.

Oh, *God*—was she nervous! She took a deep breath. She set her shoulders back. She put one foot in front of the other . . .

And then suddenly she was sitting down at the table between Mags and Jane. She had done it!

Jane raised her glass. 'To Granny Galvin,' she said. 'May she rest in peace.'

Daisy raised her glass too. 'To Granny Galvin,' she murmured.

'To Granny Galvin,' chanted the rest of the cast.

Daisy hoped she looked suitably

sad. Granny Galvin was the character who had just 'passed away'. Earlier, Daisy had asked Mags why the script writers had killed her off. The answer had been matter-of-fact. The actress who played her had been looking for too much money.

Beside her, Jane wiped away a tear. 'Poor Granny,' she said. 'Ending up in a public ward.'

Somebody sobbed. The sobbing went on until the call came from the director.

'*Cut!*' he shouted. And around the table everyone relaxed. Phones were turned on. Newspapers and magazines were opened. Mini radios and iPods were taken from pockets and handbags.

'Poor Granny,' said Jane. 'Ending up on the dole queue.'

Daisy was shocked. '*What?* Will she really have to sign on the dole?' she asked.

'Oh yes. Unless she is lucky and gets some theatre work.'

Goodness! Daisy couldn't picture little old Granny Galvin standing on the dole queue. Everyone in the country would know who she was. People would whisper. People would point. People would ask for her autograph. Signing on the dole was hard for anyone. But it must be even harder for a famous person.

Daisy looked at the famous faces at the table. There were seven of them. During the course of the morning, Daisy had learned to use the actors' real names, not their soap-opera names. She had met Patrick and James and Nick and Luke and Susie. Good old Mags and Jane felt like her new best friends at this stage. There was nothing stuck up about them. But Susie was dodgy.

Daisy found that really strange. On television, Susie came across as warm and generous. In real life she seemed anything but. When she wasn't acting she looked cross. She complained about everything.

She put on her iPod between takes so she wouldn't have to make conversation. And she ignored Daisy completely. Daisy thought it was because Susie felt it was beneath her to talk to an extra.

Daisy had also learned that most of the actors weren't at all like the gods and goddesses you saw in the magazines. They were as human as she was. Jane was worried about her little boy. Mags was scared that her hair would go frizzy. And Patrick, James, Nick and Luke were just regular guys. They swapped jokes, talked football and burped like all the guys Daisy had ever met.

From the other side of the room, the director's voice came again. 'Camera happy?'

The camera man gave the thumbs-up sign.

'Sound happy?' asked the director.

The sound man gave the thumbs-up sign.

'OK,' said the director. 'Let's move

on to the next set-up.'

Mags leaned back in her chair. 'Notice that he never asks if the actors are happy?' she remarked to Daisy.

'Why is that?'

'As long as we get our lines right and don't bump into the furniture, that's cool with him.'

'But doesn't that mean you're little more than a robot?'

'Being in a soap opera doesn't do much to get the creative juices flowing, Daisy. But sometimes even robots take control.' Mags gave a wicked smile.

'What do you mean?'

'Well, if I'm not happy with my performance, I use a rude word. Then they *have* to go for another take.'

'How clever!'

Daisy had learned lots of film stuff today. She had learned that actors never gossiped if a microphone (or a 'mic') was 'open'. If they did, they could be overheard by the sound man. She had learned about 'cheating an eyeline' and 'hitting a mark'. She had learned that 'corpsing' meant laughing when you shouldn't. And she was dying to be able to phone her mum at the end of the day and say: 'It's a wrap.'

'We're off for a fag.'

It was Nick. Daisy would know that voice anywhere. She heard it every day on radio ads. As well as acting in the soap opera, Nick got lots of work as a voice-over artist. Daisy watched as Nick and two of the younger male cast members got up. The eyes of all the female extras in the room followed them as they headed towards the door.

'Ha! If only those girls knew what dorks they are really.' Jane reached for her bag and pulled out some knitting.

Another thing Daisy had learned today was that loads of actresses knit to avoid boredom. Or did crosswords. Across the table, Patrick—the non-smoking actor— took out a pen. His *Irish Times* was open at the crossword page. Daisy watched as he started filling in clues. Holy cow—he was fast! And he was doing the difficult one. Daisy could barely manage the simple one.

Mags turned to Daisy with a smile. 'You were very good in that scene,' she told her.

'No way! All I had to do was walk across the room!'

'But you did it with great style.'

Daisy felt very proud. *Style!* Get her! 'Was I really OK?' she asked. 'I was shaking with nerves.'

'It certainly didn't show.'

'Well, thank goodness for that. Maybe I should become a pro!' Daisy smiled at Mags's alarmed expression. 'That was a joke.'

'I'm glad to hear it. Haven't you heard the Noël Coward song about going on the stage?'

'No. How does it go?'

'"The profession's overcrowded. The struggle's pretty tough,"' sang Mags. 'Those words were written seventy years ago, but they still hold true today.'

Beside her, Jane gave a great yawn. She glanced at her watch. 'Another hour until lunch,' she said. 'I wonder what mouth-watering delights are in store for us today?'

When Daisy had entered the competition, she had thought 'lunch with the cast' had sounded very grand. She had pictured linen tablecloths and silver cutlery and crystal glasses. But Mags had told her that their meal would be served on paper plates. They would be eating at a table set up in the village hall. And the chef was no Gordon Ramsay.

Mags had picked up a Staff of Life menu. 'Hey! Wish we could have lunch here. This restaurant does great seafood,' she said. 'The prices are reasonable too. Oh, yum! Look at the dessert menu. Home-made apple pie! I'd murder a slice.'

'Doesn't it seem a bit hick compared to Dublin restaurants?' asked Daisy.

'Pah! Dublin restaurants have got above themselves,' said Jane. 'And the prices are insane. I could feed my baby for a week on what some places charge for a starter.'

Across the table, Susie was clearly listening. She had finally taken off her iPod. 'I had a *fabulous* meal last night,' she said. 'There's a glorious new award-winning restaurant in Temple Bar. I had crab cakes with roasted peppers to start. And my black sole was served at the table.'

'As opposed to what? Eating it at the cooker in the kitchen?' joked Mags.

'Ha ha. Very funny,' returned Susie. 'I mean that the head waiter boned the fish at the table.'

Patrick glanced up from his crossword. 'There's a rather dodgy joke there somewhere,' he said. 'But I'm not sure you'd enjoy it, Susie.'

Susie gave him a frosty look. Then she put her headphones back on.

'I'd love to drive out here some evening and sample the food,' said Mags. 'In fact, I'd love to come for a long weekend. It would take at *least* that amount of time to recover from the stress of Dublin.'

'Don't you enjoy living in Dublin?' Daisy asked her. 'I would give anything to live there!'

Mags gave her a thoughtful look. 'I'm not sure you would,' she said. 'Don't you know how lucky you are to live in this village? It's my idea of heaven. If I got a chance to move I would jump at it.'

Daisy gave her an 'as if' look.

'Dublin has become a pretty unpleasant place to live, you know,' Jane told her. 'When was the last time you visited the Big Smoke?'

Daisy had not been to the capital since her father died. 'Three years ago,' she said.

'It's a different city today,' Mags told her. 'Traffic is at a standstill. Everyone's stressed. Shop assistants ignore you. The streets are filthy. There are no stars in the sky at night.'

'No stars? Why's that?'

'The street lamps bleach them out. Trust me, Daisy. You do not want to waste your time in Dublin.'

'But it must be so exciting to live in a city!'

'Ha! Give me village life any day! I went into your local shop earlier today for chewing gum. I was amazed when the man behind the counter thanked me for my custom. He even told me to enjoy my stay in Rosscrana! I'm definitely coming back here for a break.'

'There's not much to do here,' said Daisy. 'I mean, there are no clubs. No health spas. There isn't even a cinema!'

'Nothing to do? How about hill

walking? Horse riding? Strolling along a beach? Swimming in the sea? I could have a blast here. And I'd pig out in this restaurant every night.'

Daisy nodded at a table on the other side of the restaurant. 'Be sure to bag that window table when you come,' she said. 'The view of the sea and the harbour is lovely. Especially if there's a good sunset.'

Mags turned to look through the window. She gave a cat-like smile. 'Well, hello!' she said. 'The view is lovely right now. *Who* is the dude?'

Daisy followed her gaze. On the other side of the road, someone was leaning against the harbour wall. It was Cal Conroy.

CHAPTER FIVE

The *dude*? Surely some mistake.

'The dude?' repeated Daisy. 'That's Cal Conroy. He's not a dude.'

'My dear,' said Mags. 'That guy is *hot*. That guy could double for Johnny Depp. That guy is *a god*. How do you know him?'

'Cal? I've known him forever.' Daisy was puzzled. Cal Conroy a god?

'So he's a local, is he?' asked Mags.

'Yes.'

'Yet another reason to come here for some R & R. What does he do? No! Let me guess. Is he in a band? He has that bad-boy look.'

'No,' said Daisy. 'He is nothing as glam as that. He is only a carpenter.'

'*Only* a carpenter? What do you mean—*only* a carpenter? That is one of the sexiest jobs in the world!'

'It is?'

'For sure. Carpenters have such clever hands.'

It had never occurred to Daisy that Cal might have 'clever' hands. 'What do you mean?'

'All that carving and planing. Introduce me, why don't you?'

Daisy looked at Mags. 'Are you serious?'

'Damn right.'

Daisy turned and looked out the window again. Cal was talking on his phone. As she watched, he shook out his long black hair and stretched. His T-shirt strained against his chest. Daisy could see the outline of his pecs. Then he laughed, showing strong white teeth.

'Christ! He's gorgeous,' said Mags. 'Have you two ever . . . ?'

'*No!*' said Daisy.

'What is his work like?' asked Mags.

'I don't know,' said Daisy. 'I haven't seen any of it. He has just set up his own business.'

'Bright move.'

'You think so?'

'Absolutely. Old-fashioned trades are worth a lot in this high-tech world. Carpentry, plumbing, tailoring—all the hands-on stuff.'

Jane looked up from her needles. 'Maybe I should give up this acting lark,' she said. 'I could start making money from knitting.'

'That mightn't be a bad career move,' Mags told her. 'Did I tell you about my friend Sheila? She has set up a handwriting business.'

'Teaching handwriting?' asked Daisy.

'No, no. Writing letters for people. So many people have let their handwriting go to pot. It's because everyone is using keyboards now. She writes beautiful thank-you letters for her clients. She uses real ink and a fountain pen. And the paper is fabulous. You'd feel really special if you got a letter like that in the post. There's nothing very romantic about e-mail.'

Daisy thought about it. Mags was right. The only letters that came in through her letterbox these days were in brown envelopes. 'Funnily enough,' she said, 'I got an e-mail from Cal last night. He asked me to go for a pint some time.'

'Lucky girl! What did you—?'

But Mags never got to finish the sentence. The make-up girl came running up. The actress was needed for a close-up.

Daisy looked back at Cal. He was still talking on his phone. She remembered how she had worried last night before e-mailing him back. Cal was engaged to be married, after all. His fiancée might not like him going for a drink with Daisy. Even though they had known each other forever . . .

In the end, she had typed: 'What would your girlfriend have to say about that?'

She had received a reply in under a minute. 'Girlfriend is history. Am footloose and fiancée free.'

Daisy had worried even more. And while she worried, her Internet connection had gone dead. Cal's e-mail had not been answered.

*   *   *

'Camera happy?'

The camera man made the thumbs-up sign.

'Sound happy?'

The sound man made the thumbs-up sign.

'It's a wrap.'

The director threw his script into a recycling bin. The props people started clearing tables. The actors headed towards the village hall to change out of their costumes. Daisy's day as a television star was over.

After she had got back into her street clothes, she went looking for Ann Malone to say thank you. Ann was in the car park, thumbs flying over her BlackBerry. Behind her, actors were getting on to a coach. Patrick was still doing his crossword. Susie was still wearing her headphones. And James, Nick and Luke were hanging out of the coach windows, smoking and eyeing up the talent.

'How did you enjoy it, Daisy?' the PA asked her.

'It was the *best* day,' said Daisy. 'I'm so glad I got to hang out with Jane and Mags. They couldn't be more different from their TV characters. They're so easygoing and friendly!'

'They are. They are great girls. Hard workers, too.' Ann reached into her bag and drew out a folder. She handed it to Daisy.

'What is in this?' Daisy asked her.

'Your signed photographs of the cast,' said Ann. 'And a lovely shot of you.'

Daisy opened the folder. On the

very top of the pile of photographs was one of her. Except it didn't look like her at all. She looked so glam. Her lips were glossy. Her hair was bouncy. And her figure looked fabulous.

'Thank you so much!' said Daisy. 'My mother won't recognise me!'

Ann's BlackBerry was making noises. 'Why don't you ask Mags and Jane to write something special on their pictures for you?' she suggested. 'Here they come now. Grab them before they get on the bus.'

'Good idea.' Daisy looked in her bag for a pen.

Ann was checking out the screen on her BlackBerry. 'Excuse me, I must take this,' she said. 'Bye, Daisy!' And she moved away, talking into her phone.

Daisy waved at the actresses crossing the car park. 'Would you mind writing something nice on my photographs?' she asked.

'Of course!' said Jane.

'No problem,' said Mags. 'Wow!' she added, as she saw the picture of Daisy. 'Glamour-puss you, Daisy! Maybe you should think about becoming an actress after all.'

Daisy smiled. 'I'll stick to what I'm good at,' she said.

'Mags! Jane!' The coach driver was calling to them from across the car park. 'Get a move on! We'd all like to be in Dublin before midnight.'

The actresses stuck their tongues out at him, then finished scribbling on their photos.

'Bye, Daisy,' said Jane. She leaned towards Daisy and gave her a kiss on the cheek.

'Bye, glamour-puss!' Mags kissed her on the other cheek, then went to follow Jane across the car park. But something made her stop.

'Hey, Daisy!' she hissed over her shoulder. 'It's the hot guy!'

Cal Conroy was sitting on the car park wall. He was leaning back on his elbows. His long legs were stretched out in front of him. And he was looking at Mags with very interested eyes.

Daisy watched the actress's body language change as she walked past Cal. She started swinging her hips. She tossed her hair. And Daisy saw Cal return the lazy, meaningful smile she gave him.

With a jolt, Daisy realised she was jealous.

CHAPTER SIX

Cal turned his smile on Daisy. 'Hey, film star,' he said.

'Hey, Cal. How are things?'

'Things are good.'

Daisy moved to sit beside him on the low wall. The bus with the actors was pulling out of the car park. Mags was giving Daisy the thumbs-up sign from a window.

'How about that drink?' Cal asked her. 'You must be thirsty after your day on set.'

'All I had to do was sit at a table.'

'And walk across the room. I saw you through the window. Very nice you looked too. Did you get to keep the sexy dress?'

'Not a chance. But they gave me a picture of me in it.' Daisy slid the photo from its folder.

'Wow!' said Cal. 'That's what I'd call . . . all grown up. Is this the only shot you have?'

'Yes.'

'Shame it's not digital. I could do with new eye candy on my screen saver.'

Suddenly Daisy felt embarrassed. She grabbed the photograph from him and put it back in the folder. As she did, the signed photograph of Mags fell to the ground. Cal picked it up.

'She's a sexy girl too,' he said.

Too? What did he mean by 'too'? Did that mean he found her, Daisy, sexy? Surely not.

Cal handed her back the photograph.

He smiled at her. 'It's far from hanging around with TV stars you were reared, Daisy O'Donnell.' He put on a spoof country accent. 'Is it too big for your wellie boots you're getting? Sure, you'd never want to be seen having a pint with the likes of me.'

'A pint? No. But I'll allow you to

buy me a glass of wine, Conroy,' she said.

'Wine?' said Cal. 'I'm not sure they can run to posh stuff in the local. Will plonk do?'

Daisy got to her feet and stretched out a hand. 'Plonk is perfect. Come on, you idiot.'

*   *   *

The pub was full of elderly American tourists. They were all wearing checked trousers and drinking glasses of Guinness. There was not a woman among them. Daisy supposed the wives had gone off sight-seeing. She took a seat by the door. Cal went and got their drinks.

She started to leaf through an evening newspaper someone had left behind. It was full of boring news about the next budget. Leaf, leaf, leaf she went—until she noticed that the American tourists were whispering about her.

'Isn't that one of the actresses we saw earlier?'

'No! Is it?'

'Remember—she was the one who walked across the restaurant.'

'I think you're right!'

'Hey! Neat!'

'Ask her for her autograph!'

'No. It's rude to intrude. She's here for a quiet drink with her boyfriend.'

Her *boyfriend*! Daisy nearly laughed out loud.

She looked up as Cal set a glass on the table in front of her. His eyes were very green. How had she never noticed that about him before? 'Your wine, madam,' he said.

'Thanks.' Daisy set down the paper and glanced at the tourists. 'Cal?'

'Yes?'

'They think I'm famous.'

'Who thinks you're famous? Those Yanks?'

'Yes. I saw them peering through the Staff of Life window when we were filming. They think I'm one of the cast members. They're talking about asking me for my autograph.'

'Cool!'

Daisy took a sip of her wine. 'No. It's not cool. They'll be in for a big let down,' she said.

'Why?'

'When they find out I'm only an extra, of course. They'll be dead disappointed.'

'Then don't tell them.'

'What? And pretend I'm a soap-opera star?'

'Why not?'

'Because it's dishonest.'

'Who cares? They're not going to know any better. And you'll make their day. There's no harm in making a bunch of old people happy.'

A small cough made Daisy look up. One of the Americans was standing at the table. 'Excuse me, miss?' he said. 'Could I ask you to sign this for me?' He held out a beermat.

Daisy was just about to say: 'I'm sorry, I'm not who you think I am.' But Cal was too quick.

'She'd be delighted to,' he told the American. 'Wouldn't you, Daisy?'

'Daisy!' said the American with a big smile. 'What a cute name!' He turned to his friends. 'She's called Daisy!'

'Hi, Daisy!'

'Great to meet you!'

'Mind if we join you?'

'Can we buy you a drink?'

And within minutes Daisy was surrounded by a circle of elderly admirers. They shook her hand. They brought more beermats to be signed. And they treated Daisy and Cal to another round of drinks.

It turned out that they were a bunch of ex-pat Irishmen who had all been widowed. One of them had set up a support group on the Internet and together they had learned how to live life after loss. They booked themselves into hotels for poker weekends. They went whale watching. And now they were touring Ireland.

'We were in Dublin yesterday,' one of them told her. 'We couldn't get out of there fast enough. You are so lucky to live in this pretty village. It is my idea of heaven.'

Funny. That was the second time someone had said that to her today.

'You remind me of my wife when she was young,' said another of the group. 'Would you care to see a picture?'

'I'd love to,' said Daisy.

The man took a picture from his wallet. It was of a pretty redhead wearing a dress in the same colour chiffon as the one Daisy had worn today.

'It was taken on our honeymoon,' said the man.

'She's beautiful,' said Daisy. 'And she has such kind eyes. You must miss her very much.'

'I never stop missing her.' The

man took one more look at the photo of his wife before putting it back into his wallet.

'I have a photo of my wife, too,' said another of the men.

'So have I.'

'And here's mine,' said a man with a shy face. 'It was taken on the first night we kissed. I'll never forget it.'

Photograph after photograph was passed from hand to hand. And as Daisy looked at the smiling faces of their loved ones, she was reminded of her dad. There was a photograph of him by her mother's bed. She knew how very, very tough her mum's life was without him. Daisy's heart filled with sympathy for these strangers.

An hour or so later, the tourist bus pulled up outside the pub. It was time for the men to take off on the next leg of their trip. But first there were photos to be taken of Daisy with each of them. Her cheek was kissed over and over. Her shoulders were sore from the weight of the arms that had been hung round them. Finally she posed for a shot with Cal.

'Smile!' the men told her.

'Put your arm around her,' said one.

'Give her a kiss!' said another. And before she knew what was happening, Cal was kissing her long and hard. Daisy had never been kissed by an expert before. The effect it had on her was electric.

A cheer went up. When Cal finally broke the kiss, Daisy sank down onto her seat feeling dizzy. Was she dizzy because of Cal? Or was the wine she had drunk to blame?

She watched as the men left the pub, calling out goodbyes. The last man out was the man with the shy face, the one who would never forget the first time he had kissed his wife. 'Goodbye, love's young dream!' he said with a smile. 'I'll be sure to send you a copy of the photo!' And then he disappeared through the door, leaving Cal and Daisy staring at each other.

'Well. How the hell did that happen?' said Cal.

CHAPTER SEVEN

How the hell *had* that happened? Daisy hadn't a clue. Nor did she have a clue what to say. Thankfully, she was saved by the bell. Her mobile rang. It was her mother, wanting to know how her day as a TV star had gone.

'Fine!' said Daisy. 'I'm on my way home now.' She ended the call, then threw her phone back in her bag. 'I have to go,' she said to Cal. She didn't—*couldn't*—meet his eyes. 'I'll see you around.' She ran from the pub without looking back at him. She was glad that he could not see her face. She knew it had gone bright red. And she knew the redness wasn't because of the wine she had drunk.

At home, her mother was in good form. There was pasta in the oven and a green salad on the table.

'Mam?' Daisy asked. 'Would you mind if I took a day off tomorrow?'

'Not at all,' said her mother. 'The order book is empty. What are you planning on doing?'

'I want to go to Dublin,' said Daisy.

*   *   *

Daisy didn't really want to go anywhere. But she needed to put distance between herself and Rosscrana. She needed time to think.

The bus from Rosscrana took her to Dublin city centre. From there, she walked across O'Connell Bridge to Grafton Street. She wanted to check out the capital's coolest shopping street. She wanted to see what she was missing.

At the bottom of Grafton Street stood a living statue. She was wearing golden robes and a golden wig. Her skin was painted gold too. Daisy dropped a coin into the box at her feet. The golden girl blew a kiss at her. On a corner a man with a guitar was singing 'Dublin Can Be Heaven'. Across from him a street trader was selling wooden puppets.

Dublin can be heaven!

A little further up Grafton Street, Daisy stopped in front of a window display. It was like a scene from a fairytale. On a pedestal in the middle of the display was an elegant dummy. The train of the dummy's gown was made from yards and *yards* of silk. It fell down like a waterfall and pooled on the floor. On this silk carpet, treasure had been scattered. Boxes, crates and chests all spilled beautiful objects. There were tiaras and bracelets and jewelled collars. There were bags covered in beads and bags covered in feathers. There were glossy leather shoes and pretty satin slippers. There were hats as big as cartwheels and hats smaller than Daisy's hand. There were items of underwear covered in roses and lace and ribbons. The display lured Daisy inside.

But inside was a different story. The end-of-season sale was on, Daisy realised. The place was like a rugby scrum. People were pushing. People were grabbing. It was horrible. After she had been poked in the ribs for the third time, Daisy decided it was time to get out.

But outside was just as bad.

Dublin can be heaven? Daisy was beginning to wonder. Grafton Street was full now with people on their lunch breaks. They moved fast. Daisy found herself ducking and diving. Every time she got in someone's way, her apology was greeted with a snarl. Every time she held a door open, people streamed past without saying thank you. Every second person was on the phone. 'I'm coming down Grafton Street!' they shouted. Or 'I'm going up Grafton Street!' they yelled. Music blared from shops. A street sweeper sprayed dust and noise. Slogans on T-shirts read 'You suck', 'I love shopping' and 'He with the most toys wins'.

Daisy wandered in and out of trendy shops. The clothes were the same in every single one. Gum-chewing girls pulled dresses and tops off rails. They held them up, gave them the once over, then let them drop. They pushed each other and gave each other nasty looks. Skinny shop assistants acted bored. Big bouncers looked mean and muttered into mouthpieces. Nobody was smiling.

Daisy suddenly found the *pointlessness* of everything depressing. There was a lot on display, but that was all it was. *Display.* For show. There was nothing she wanted to buy. She longed to see a friendly face. She had had enough. Her head throbbed, her feet were killing her and she badly needed some coffee.

In a café, she found a table by a window and ordered a coffee and a wrap. The coffee was all foam and no taste. The wrap could have been made from cardboard. Across the road, a woman was collecting for famine relief. She was shaking a bucket with a charity's name on it. Daisy watched as the people swept past her. Women walked past in stupid pointy-toed shoes. Most of them had expensive hair-dos and bags with designer logos. Men kept their hands in the pockets of their well-cut suits. None of them bothered to throw some change into the famine relief bucket. Not a single coin was offered.

Daisy recalled the images she saw on television night after night. The babies with huge hopeless eyes. The mothers with empty breasts. The fathers sitting in the dust. The images always made her cry. Now she felt like crying even more.

A celebrity was making his way down Grafton Street. He looked as if he was walking up the red carpet at a film premiere. He smiled at the fans who recognised him, showing very white teeth. His shirt was open, displaying a tanned chest. He stopped to sign an autograph for a teenage fan. Then he too walked past the woman collecting money for famine relief.

Daisy had had enough. She wanted to go home. She paid and left a tip for the waitress. Then she went straight across the street and dropped all her change into the bucket. The woman looked at her gratefully. 'Thank you so much,' she said. 'I've been standing here for nearly forty minutes. You're the first person who has given me anything.'

*   *   *

Once she had made herself comfortable on the bus home to Rosscrana, Daisy found herself thinking about Cal. Something made

67

her compare him with the celebrity she had seen on Grafton Street today. The celebrity was meant to be a national sex symbol, but there had been nothing sexy about his smile. It hadn't reached his eyes. Cal's eyes were always smiling. She remembered how he had smiled at her after he had kissed her. And then she found herself dreaming about when he might kiss her again and how she would feel if he did . . .

The driver woke her when they reached Rosscrana. When she got off the bus she felt like Dorothy after her adventures in *The Wizard of Oz*. And just as Dorothy had done when she was safely back in Kansas, Daisy said to herself, 'There's no place like home.'

Behind her a voice said, 'You know what they say about girls who talk to themselves?'

She turned to see Cal looking down at her. There was something about the way he was regarding her.

'What do they say?' she asked him.

His lips curved in a smile. 'They say they have a strong fantasy life. Is that how you spent your bus journey? In fantasy land?'

'No,' she lied. She knew she had gone very red.

Cal reached out and took her hand. 'Let's go for a stroll,' he said.

In silence, they walked down the main street of the village. At the end of the street, Cal took a left. This path would lead them to the beach. Rosscrana was famous for this stretch of golden strand.

There was a light wind blowing. It ruffled the waves on the sea. The setting sun shone on the dunes. There was a tangy smell of seaweed. Little black and white birds ran along the water's edge, searching for worms. A mile high in the sky, a skylark was singing. To the east, the evening star was rising. Daisy had read somewhere that the evening star was the planet Venus.

'What were you doing in Dublin?' Cal asked her.

'I guess I wanted to see if the grass really is greener there.'

'Very little grass grows in the city.'

She smiled up at him. 'I know. And what grass does grow there isn't green at all. It's dusty and dry. No sheep could graze there.'

'Apart from Bono's. In Stephen's Green.'

She gave him an 'as if' look. 'Are you winding me up, Conroy?'

'No word of a lie. It's an ancient by-law. He's allowed to do that now U2 has the Freedom of the City.'

'Cool!'

They walked down to the water's edge, then kicked their shoes off. The water round their ankles was clear.

'You've always wanted a life in the city, Daisy,' said Cal.

'I know. And I might have had one if Dad hadn't died. I could be there now, one of those stressed out city girls. Commuting to a tiny apartment. Never hearing birdsong. Never looking up at night to see stars in the sky. Instead I have all this on my doorstep.' Daisy's gesture took in the sand, the sea and the sky. She looked sideways at Cal. 'And so have you. I understand you're back for good?'

'I am.'

'What happened to the fiancée?'

'Nothing happened. She was a career girl. She couldn't have stayed here any more than I could have stayed on in London.' Cal put his hands in his pockets. He looked relaxed. 'I suggest we change the subject.'

'OK. What do you want to talk about?'

'Statistics,' he said. 'Statistics prove that at any given time—'

Daisy interrupted him. 'Statistics?' she said. 'You're surely not going to bore me with *statistics* on a beautiful evening like this, Cal!'

'Allow me to finish.' He cleared his throat. 'Statistics prove that at any given time a boy and a girl on a beach somewhere in the world are kissing. Did you know that?'

Daisy shook her head.

'Did you enjoy it?' he asked. 'When we kissed last night?'

Daisy looked down at her feet. She wiggled her toes and felt sand between them. 'I enjoyed it,' she said.

'In that case,' said Cal, 'if a boy and a girl are to kiss on a beach right now, it may as well be this beach. Can I kiss you again, Daisy?'

Daisy smiled. She was remembering the dream she had had on the bus. About when Cal might kiss her again and how she would feel if he did . . .

'Yes, please, Cal,' she said. 'I think I would like that very much.'

He moved towards her and took her in his arms. He lifted her hand and kissed all five fingers. He stroked her face and pushed back a strand of hair. He smiled at her with his eyes. And then he lowered his mouth to hers.

Behind closed eyes, Daisy O'Donnell found herself gazing at stars. The reality was far, far better than the dream.